D1275183

Studio Fun International
An imprint of Printers Row Publishing Group
A division of Readerlink Distribution Services, LLC
10350 Barnes Canyon Road, Suite 100, San Diego, CA 92121
www.studiofun.com

MARVEL

Printers Row Publishing Group is a division of Readerlink Distribution Services, LLC.
Studio Fun International is a registered trademark of Readerlink Distribution Services, LLC.

All notations of errors or omissions should be addressed to Studio Fun International, Editorial Department, at the above address.

ISBN: 978-0-7944-4676-5
Manufactured, printed, and assembled in Heshan, China.
First printing, November 2020. HH/11/20
24 23 22 21 20   1 2 3 4 5

Clint Barton was enjoying an afternoon with his family. His daughter, Lila, was learning how to use a bow and arrow, just like her dad. Behind them, his wife and sons were getting ready for a picnic.

Lila pointed her toes and, when she was ready, let go of the arrow. Bull's-eye.

"Good job, Hawkeye," Clint said proudly. "Go get your arrow."

Clint looked away for a moment. When he turned around, Lila was no longer there. Nor was the rest of his family. They had simply disappeared.

Thousands of miles away, in outer space, Tony Stark and Nebula were trying to return to Earth in the Guardians of the Galaxy's spaceship. The ship had been damaged during the battle with Thanos. Working together, they were able to keep it flying for a couple of days.

But now their luck had run out.

"This thing on?" Tony joked, as he started recording a message with his Iron Man helmet. "Hey, Miss Potts. Pep. If you find this recording, don't post it on social media. It's gonna be a real tearjerker."

In a calm voice, he told Pepper Potts that their oxygen would soon run out. "Pep, I know I said no more surprises, but I gotta say I was really hoping to pull off one last one."

He finished the message to her, and then fell asleep. A short while later, he woke to a bright light beaming in through the cockpit. A person was floating outside the ship!

On Earth, the surviving Avengers were gathered at their headquarters. Suddenly, the building started to shake!

Steve Rogers, Natasha Romanoff, Bruce Banner, and James Rhodes raced outside. They saw Captain Marvel guiding a spaceship with her hands. She gently lowered it to the ground.

The ship's hatch opened. Steve ran over to help his friend Tony down the steps.

"I lost the kid," Tony confessed. Steve knew that he meant Peter Parker.

—The team headed into Avengers Headquarters and straight to the briefing room. Video screens flashed images of the missing Avengers— the ones who had disappeared when Thanos snapped his fingers with the Infinity Gauntlet.

Steve wanted to locate Thanos and find a way to reverse the Blip. Tony didn't believe that was possible.

While Tony rested, the Avengers gathered with Nebula and Rocket. Nebula thought she knew where Thanos might be.

Thanos had told Nebula that when his plan was finished, he would go to the garden.

With a little help from Rocket, the Avengers were able to trace the energy from the Infinity Gauntlet. They found a planet where Thanos had recently used it.

Armed with the coordinates, the Avengers boarded the Guardians' ship to confront Thanos.

"Okay," Rocket said, sounding like a schoolteacher. "Who here hasn't been to space?"

Captain America, War Machine, and Black Widow raised their hands.

The ship passed through a jump point in space and arrived at the garden planet.

"I'll head down for recon," Captain Marvel announced as she exited the ship.

Captain Marvel finished her scan of the garden planet and found nothing.

"No satellites," she told them over the ship's speakers. "No ships. No armies. No ground defenses of any kind. It's just him."

"And that's enough," Nebula said seriously.

On the planet below, Thanos was tending to his garden. He had hung his armor on a post—making a giant scarecrow.

Thanos gathered some fruit and slowly walked to his small hut.

The Avengers took Thanos by surprise. Captain Marvel, War Machine, and Hulk held the villain in a tight grip while Rocket examined the Infinity Gauntlet. The Infinity Stones were missing.

Thanos admitted he had destroyed the stones so he wouldn't be tempted to use the gauntlet again. That meant there was no way to bring everyone back.

In a fit of rage, Thor brought his axe, Stormbreaker, down on Thanos.

Five years had passed since Thanos snapped his fingers. The Avengers were trying to move on. Natasha was debriefing the team using hologram technology.

"Carol, are we seeing you here next month?" Natasha asked Captain Marvel.

"Not likely," Carol replied. "I'm covering a lot of territory. The things that are happening on Earth are happening everywhere. On thousands of planets."

"Well, this channel's always active," Natasha said.

All the holograms disappeared, except for War Machine. He was keeping track of Clint Barton, who had gone underground since the Blip. Rhodey promised to tell Natasha when he found out where Clint was going next.

Steve Rogers walked into the briefing room. Natasha and Steve were talking when they noticed someone at the security gate.

It was Scott Lang—Ant-Man. But they thought he had disappeared in the Blip!

Scott explained that he had been trapped in the Quantum Realm for five years, but it felt like five hours to him.

"Time works differently in the Quantum Realm," Scott told them. "The only problem is right now we don't have a way to navigate it. But what if we did?"

"Are you talking about a time machine?" Steve asked.

"I know, it's crazy," Scott admitted.

"I get e-mails from a raccoon," Natasha said. "Nothing sounds crazy anymore."

  With the beginnings of a plan, Steve, Natasha, and Scott went to Tony
first. They wanted to see if he would come back to the team and help plan
what Scott called a "Time Heist."

  Tony refused. He and Pepper were married now. They had a little girl
named Morgan. Tony didn't want to risk losing what he had.

So they met with Bruce Banner, who was now the Hulk, but with Banner's mind! They asked Bruce what he thought about their plan.

"The whole time-travel do-over?" Bruce wondered, unsure. "Ah, guys, it's outside my area of expertise."

But he couldn't say no to his friends.

"Okay, here we go!" Bruce said. "Time travel test number one!"

Scott Lang, wearing the Ant-Man suit, jumped into the Quantum Tunnel. When he came out, he was twelve years old.

Ant-Man jumped in again and reappeared as an old man. He went back into the Quantum Tunnel and emerged as a baby. Finally, he returned at just the right age.

"Time travel!" Bruce shouted with glee.

Steve wasn't sure if their plan was going to work. He took a walk outside Avengers Headquarters. Tony pulled up and told Steve that he had solved the problem with time travel.

Then he gave Steve his shield.

"Will you keep that a little quiet?" Tony teased, pointing at the shield. "Didn't bring one for the whole team."

With Rocket's help, Tony constructed a large Quantum Platform. The plan was simple: Split into teams, travel back in time to retrieve the six Infinity Stones, and return them to the present. Then they could snap their fingers and bring everyone back!

"You know your teams," Captain America said to the Avengers. "You know your missions. Get the Stones. No mistakes. No do-overs."

Cap looked at his teammates. "Look out for each other. This is the fight of our lives. And we're gonna win. Whatever it takes. Good luck."

Rocket looked at Ant-Man and commented, "He's pretty good at that."

Hulk flipped the switches, and soon the Avengers were traveling back in time.

Captain America, Iron Man, Hulk, and Ant-Man arrived in New York City in the year 2012. They needed to get the Space Stone and the Mind Stone—both of which would be at Stark Tower. Captain America, Iron Man, and Ant-Man would go after those. Hulk would get the Time Stone, which was located at Doctor Strange's Sanctum Sanctorum.

At Stark Tower, everything was going according to plan until Tony lost the Space Stone. Captain America had the Mind Stone, but then he ran into . . . himself!

It was Steve Rogers from 2012!

The two fought, and Captain America managed to defeat his past self.

He met Iron Man and Ant-Man outside. They needed a new plan to get the Space Stone.

Captain America and Iron Man made a plan to find the Space Stone at S.H.I.E.L.D. in 1970. It was risky; if their plan didn't work, they would be stuck in the past. But they knew they had to try.

Meanwhile, Hulk arrived at the Sanctum Sanctorum. But Doctor Strange wasn't there—he wouldn't become a master of the mystic arts for another couple of years! Hulk explained to the Ancient One why he needed the Time Stone.

The Ancient One agreed to give him the Stone, but only if Hulk promised to bring it back to the exact moment he borrowed it.

Meanwhile, Thor and Rocket had arrived in Asgard in the year 2013. Rocket had no trouble getting the Reality Stone. But then Thor ran into his mother! He had missed her so much after she died.

The two heroes were just about to return to the present when Thor extended his hand. A moment later, his hammer Mjolnir appeared. Thor was happy to be reunited with his weapon.

In the year 2014, War Machine and Nebula were on Morag. They watched as Black Widow and Hawkeye left for Vormir in the Guardians' ship. War Machine and Nebula were after an object called the Orb, which contained the Power Stone.

Nebula didn't know it, but she shared a cybernetic link with Nebula from 2014. That Nebula still hated her sister, Gamora, and would do anything to help her father, Thanos.

With Ebony Maw's help, Thanos of 2014 was able to search present-day Nebula's memories for the Infinity Stones.

He watched one hologram of the future Thanos confronting the Avengers, and another of the Avengers planning their time heist.

Thanos saw that he would collect the Infinity Stones in the future and succeed in wiping out half the universe.

Now he also knew that the Avengers would travel through time to get the Stones and undo his work. Thanos came up with a new plan.

He boarded the *Sanctuary II* and traveled to Morag to kidnap present-day Nebula.

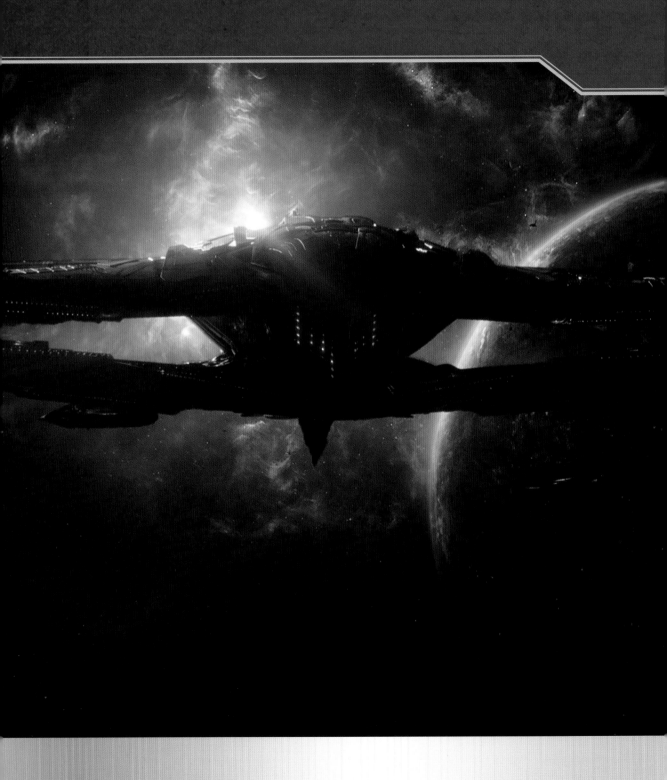

On the planet Vormir, Black Widow and Hawkeye climbed a mountain in search of the Soul Stone. When they reached the top, they found an eerie, floating figure.

"What you seek lies in front of you," the figure said solemnly. "As does what you fear."

Black Widow and Hawkeye looked over the cliff's edge. The Soul Stone was below them.

The figure warned them, "In order to take the Stone you must lose that which you love. An everlasting exchange. A soul for a soul."

Both Hawkeye and Black Widow knew what had to be done.

"Whatever it takes," Black Widow said, echoing Captain America's words.

Hawkeye looked over the edge of the tower. "Whatever it takes," he repeated.

Both Avengers were willing to sacrifice themselves to help bring back countless lives. But in the end, it was Black Widow who gave her life for trillions.

The Avengers had done it. They had successfully collected the six Infinity Stones.

When they returned to the present, Captain America looked around. He saw that everyone had made it back—everyone except Black Widow.

Captain America lowered his head as Hulk collapsed to his knees.

"She sacrificed her life for that Stone," Clint said quietly. "She bet her life on it."

"We have to make it worth it," Bruce insisted. "We have to."

Steve rose to his feet. "We will," he promised.

Tony and Rocket went to work in the lab. Mechanical arms carefully placed the six Infinity Stones into a specially made gauntlet. It surged with energy.

"All right," Rocket declared. "The glove's ready. Question is, who's gonna snap their freakin' fingers?"

Hulk stepped up. "It's gotta be me," he stated. "You saw what those Stones did to Thanos. They almost killed him. None of you could survive."

Hulk slowly put his hand into the gauntlet and said, "Everybody comes home."

Then the Infinity Stones began to glow. Hulk grunted in pain as the energy pulsed through his body.

He screamed.

"Bruce, are you okay?" Captain America shouted.

Energy flowed through Hulk's right arm, burning his skin. He gritted his teeth and said, "I'm okay!"

Nobody knew quite what would happen. Iron Man activated shields in the lab in case something went wrong. The other Avengers were wearing their gear, ready for anything.

Hulk screamed in pain. With great effort, he raised his right hand and snapped his fingers.

The universe went blank.

There was one Avenger who wasn't in the lab with the others—because she wasn't really an Avenger. The Nebula who returned to the present was really the Nebula from 2014.

She snuck into the hangar and activated the Quantum Tunnel Platform.

A moment later, the *Sanctuary II* from 2014 arrived!

Thanos was aboard the massive ship with Gamora from 2014 and the present-day Nebula. The ship hovered above Avengers Headquarters and unleashed a barrage of missiles, destroying it—with the Avengers still inside.

At first, no one knew what hit them. Rocket, Rhodey, and Hulk were trapped underground beneath tons of rubble. Hulk used his incredible strength to uncover them while they waited for Ant-Man to get them out.

Meanwhile, Hawkeye found himself in an underground tunnel. The gauntlet was right beside him. He picked it up and ran!

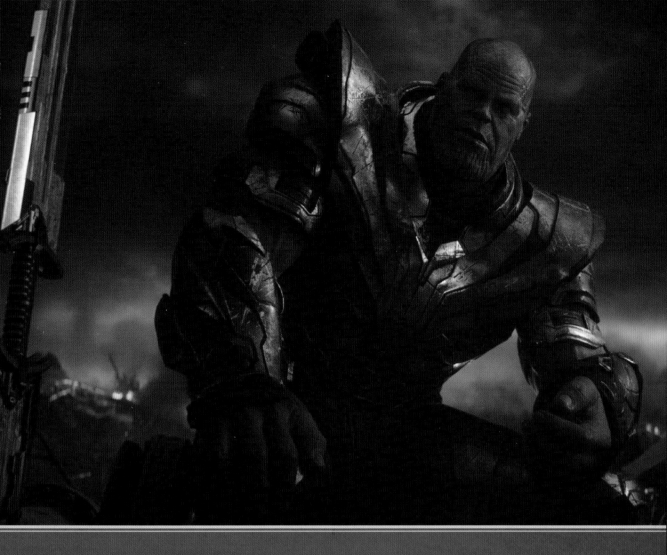

    Captain America looked around, surveying the damage.
"What happened?"
    "You mess with time, it tends to mess back," Iron Man said.
    They crawled out of the rubble and found Thor—and Thanos.
Together, the three heroes bravely walked toward their foe.
    Thanos told them how he would take the new gauntlet and snap
his fingers again. This time, he would destroy all life in the universe,
and create a new universe of beings.

Iron Man knew they had to keep the gauntlet away from Thanos. The best way to do that was to attack him.

He unleashed the full might of his Iron Man armor on the villain. Thor supercharged the armor with lightning blasts. But Thanos tossed Iron Man aside like a doll.

Thor swung at Thanos with Stormbreaker, but the villain blocked it.

Then Thor's hammer Mjolnir soared through the air—but it didn't go to Thor's hand. Instead, it traveled to Captain America. He was worthy!

"I knew it!" Thor shouted, proud to see his friend wielding Mjolnir.

Thanos was stunned as Captain America came at him twirling the powerful hammer. Leaping into the air, Cap pounded Thanos. The villain crashed to the ground!

Using the hammer and his shield, Cap continued his attack. Thanos was shocked by the sudden onslaught.

Slowly, Thanos got back to his feet, and smashed Cap's supposedly unbreakable shield to pieces.

Now Thanos was angry. "In all my years of conquest, it was never personal," Thanos admitted. "But I'll tell you now, what I'm about to do to your stubborn, annoying little planet, I'm gonna enjoy very, very much."

Sanctuary II beamed Cull Obsidian, Corvus Glaive, Proxima Midnight, and Ebony Maw to the ground below—along with Outriders, the Chitauri, tanks, and weapons.

Only Captain America was left standing to stop them.

Suddenly, a voice came over Steve's communications link.

"Cap, it's Sam. Can you hear me?"

Captain America smiled as Sam Wilson—Falcon—soared through a glowing portal that had opened behind him.

"On your left!" Falcon shouted to his friend. Cap saw Black Panther, Shuri, Okoye, and the armies of Wakanda coming out of the portal.

More portals opened and Doctor Strange and Wong, Star-Lord, Drax, Mantis, Spider-Man, Scarlet Witch, Winter Soldier, and more appeared.

Hulk's snap had worked! They had brought everyone back!

Now, two massive armies faced off against each other in a battle for the fate of the universe.

"Avengers assemble!" Captain America called out.

Thanos's army was fearsome, but the heroes had the upper hand.

Hawkeye emerged from the ruined tunnels beneath Avengers Headquarters carrying the gauntlet. Thanos's army went after him—desperate to get the gauntlet for their master.

Hawkeye hurled the gauntlet to Black Panther, who tried to keep it from Ebony Maw. Maw used his telekinetic powers to trap Black Panther.

"I got it!" Spider-Man yelled, spinning a web line to pull the gauntlet out of Black Panther's hands.

The heroes were winning—and that was something Thanos could not allow. He ordered his ship to fire at the battlefield, with no regard for who they hit! Exploding missiles took out everything—even members of Thanos's army—in hopes that they would destroy the heroes.

But then something streaked across the sky. "Is anyone else seeing this?" Pepper asked.

The blip of light flew right into the *Sanctuary II* and smashed through its hull. The light flew around and smashed through the ship again. Captain Marvel had arrived!

The *Sanctuary II* crashed to the ground below.

Thanos clenched his teeth in anger.

Thanos's army was closing in on Spider-Man—and the gauntlet.
"Danvers, we need an assist here!" Captain America called out.
Captain Marvel got the message, and landed right next to Spider-Man.
"Hi, I'm Peter Parker," he introduced himself politely.
"Hey, Peter Parker," Captain Marvel responded. "You got something for me?"
Spider-Man gave her the gauntlet. Then Ant-Man and Wasp readied the Quantum Tunnel to send the gauntlet back in time!

Spider-Man watched as Thanos's army approached. A horde of Chitauri and Outriders were heading their way, followed by Corvus Glaive and Proxima Midnight.

"I don't know how you're gonna get it through all of that," Spider-Man said.

Captain Marvel smiled.

"Don't worry," Scarlet Witch assured Spider-Man.
"She's got help," Okoye added.
Suddenly, Captain Marvel was joined by an army of Super Heroes.
Corvus Glaive and Proxima Midnight charged at the Avengers, but they were instantly repelled.

Thanos hurled his blade at the Quantum Tunnel just before Captain Marvel could get to it with the gauntlet. The Tunnel exploded. Captain Marvel was knocked to the ground, and she dropped the gauntlet.

Iron Man walked through the rubble. He could see the gauntlet on the ground. Before he could grab it, Thanos appeared.

Iron Man attacked Thanos, but the giant villain threw him to the ground.

Thor and Captain America tried to stop Thanos, but he was merciless. He defeated them both. At long last, Thanos picked up his prize and admired it.

There was no one to stop Thanos from using the gauntlet and wiping out the entire universe!

Thanos put on the gauntlet and felt the surge of power. Just as he was about to bring the thumb and middle finger together, Captain Marvel flew toward the villain. She grabbed at the gauntlet and pulled Thanos's hand down.

Thanos screamed as Captain Marvel used her photon-enhanced strength to keep him from snapping his fingers. He groaned as he tried to free his hand. With great effort and the help of the Power Stone, Thanos escaped Captain Marvel's grasp.

Iron Man threw himself at Thanos to grab the gauntlet. But Thanos hurled him to the ground.

    With a smirk, Thanos showed Iron Man the gauntlet and said, "I am inevitable."

    Then he snapped his fingers.

    The snap made a metallic sound, and the Avengers waited for everything to disappear.

    But that didn't happen. In fact, nothing happened!

Thanos looked at the gauntlet and turned it over to look at the Stones. The Stones were gone!

Iron Man raised his right hand, revealing all six Infinity Stones. When he was grappling with Thanos, Iron Man had removed the Stones from the gauntlet. Thanos watched in horror as they drifted across Iron Man's armor and settled into his Iron Man gauntlet. Energy surged through Iron Man's body, and the Stones began to glow.

Iron Man locked eyes with Thanos and announced proudly,
"And I . . . am . . . Iron Man."
Holding his hand up, the Super Hero snapped his fingers.
It was immediately clear to Thanos what Iron Man had done.
He watched as his army turned into dust. The fate he had planned
for the universe now belonged to him and his minions.

Captain America looked at Thanos, watching as the Titan sat down to accept his fate. A moment later, Thanos disappeared.

The Avengers had won. But the victory came at a tremendous price.

The gauntlet's tremendous power had wounded Iron Man badly. In the end, he took his last breath with Pepper by his side.

Tony's closest companions gathered on the dock behind his lake house to pay their respects.

Pepper and Morgan walked down the dock, followed by Steve, Rhodey, and their friend Happy Hogan. Behind them, the Avengers had assembled once more.

Pepper placed flowers on the lake. Tony's very first arc reactor rested in the center of the bouquet. Around the reactor, Pepper had made a sign that read simply, "Proof that Tony Stark has a heart."

After Iron Man's funeral, the Avengers went their separate ways.

Thor returned to New Asgard and pronounced Valkyrie as the new ruler of the kingdom.

He turned to see the Guardians' ship parked in a field nearby. Rocket waved.

"Move it or lose it, hairbag," Rocket said.

Thor left with Rocket to join the Guardians of the Galaxy on their next adventure.

Bruce Banner, Sam, and Bucky stood outside the demolished Avengers Headquarters. Bruce was working the controls of a new Quantum Tunnel.

"Remember, you have to return the Stones to the exact moment you got 'em," Bruce warned.

Captain America smiled as he picked up the case holding the Infinity Stones and Thor's hammer.

"You know, if you want, I could come with you," Sam offered.

"You're a good man, Sam. This one's on me, though," Cap said, then disappeared in the Quantum Tunnel.

The moment Steve should have returned from the past came and went.
"Get him back!" Sam cried.
Then Bucky pointed toward the lake. A man sat quietly on a bench.
"Go ahead," Bucky urged Sam.

The man on the bench was Steve—a much older Steve. He told Sam that he had decided to stay in the past and had lived a full life.

He handed his shield to Sam.

Sam took the shield and accepted its responsibility. "Thank you. I'll do my best," Sam said.

Steve shook Sam's hand. "That's why it's yours," Steve said. He had faith in his friend.